THIS BOOK BELONGS TO

_____

# ERICK'S HUNGRY WINTER

## BY LOIS L. SANDO

### ILLUSTRATED BY TAMMIE LANE

November 2002

To Deanna —

May Erick find a place
in your heart & on your bookshelf

Lois L. Sando

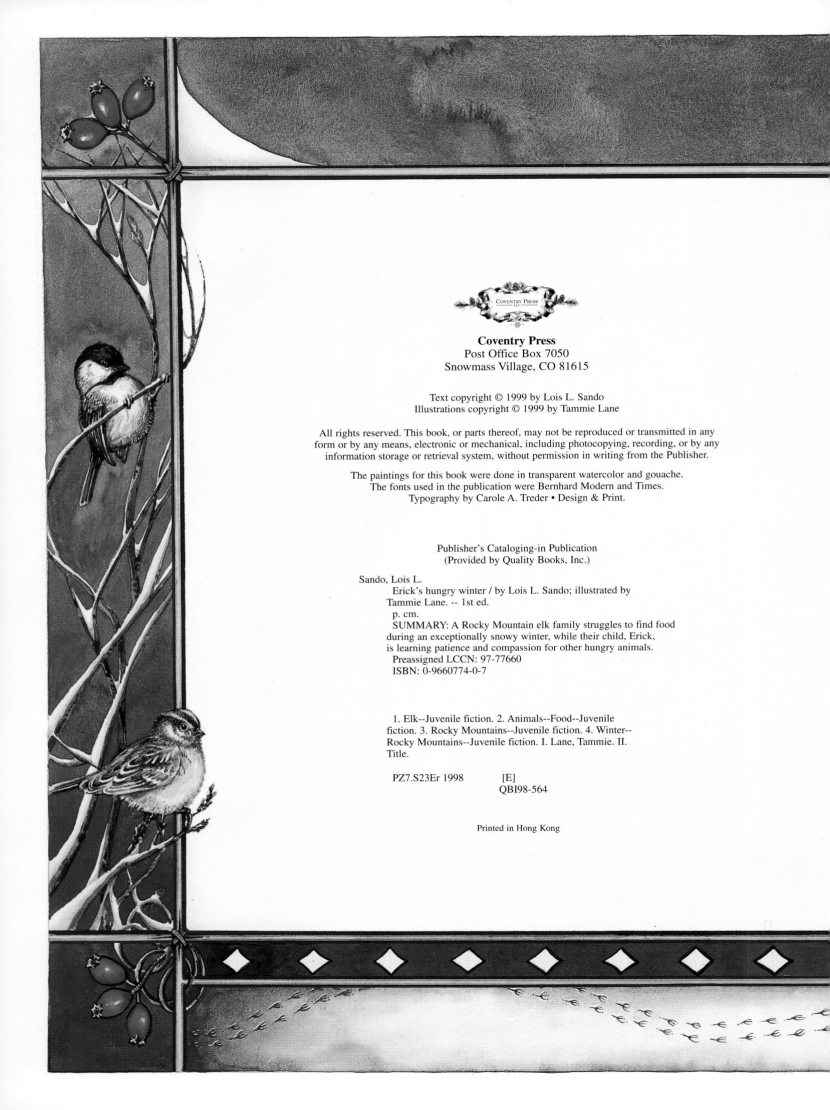

**Coventry Press**
Post Office Box 7050
Snowmass Village, CO 81615

The paintings for this book were done in transparent watercolor and gouache.
The fonts used in the publication were Bernhard Modern and Times.
Typography by Carole A. Treder • Design & Print.

Publisher's Cataloging-in Publication
(Provided by Quality Books, Inc.)

Sando, Lois L.
    Erick's hungry winter / by Lois L. Sando; illustrated by
Tammie Lane. -- 1st ed.
    p. cm.
    SUMMARY: A Rocky Mountain elk family struggles to find food
during an exceptionally snowy winter, while their child, Erick,
is learning patience and compassion for other hungry animals.
    Preassigned LCCN: 97-77660
    ISBN: 0-9660774-0-7

    1. Elk--Juvenile fiction. 2. Animals--Food--Juvenile
fiction. 3. Rocky Mountains--Juvenile fiction. 4. Winter--
Rocky Mountains--Juvenile fiction. I. Lane, Tammie. II.
Title.

PZ7.S23Er 1998          [E]
                        QBI98-564

Printed in Hong Kong

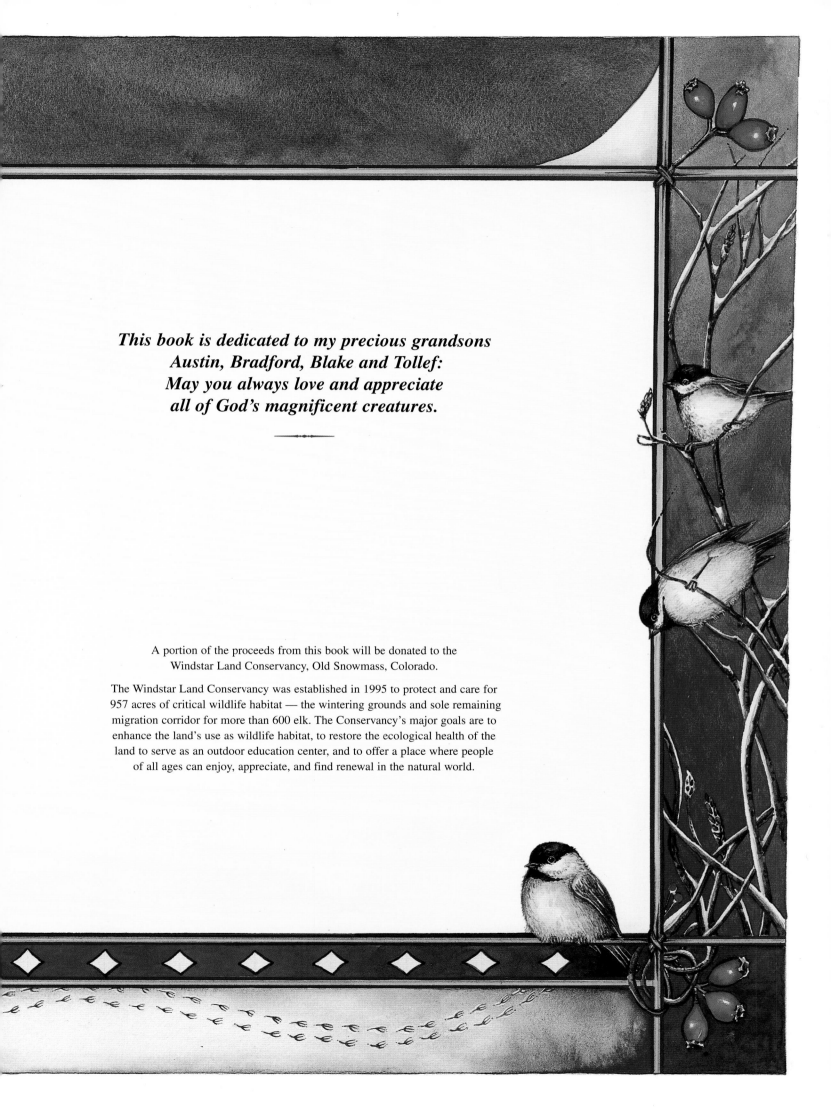

*This book is dedicated to my precious grandsons
Austin, Bradford, Blake and Tollef:
May you always love and appreciate
all of God's magnificent creatures.*

A portion of the proceeds from this book will be donated to the
Windstar Land Conservancy, Old Snowmass, Colorado.

The Windstar Land Conservancy was established in 1995 to protect and care for
957 acres of critical wildlife habitat — the wintering grounds and sole remaining
migration corridor for more than 600 elk. The Conservancy's major goals are to
enhance the land's use as wildlife habitat, to restore the ecological health of the
land to serve as an outdoor education center, and to offer a place where people
of all ages can enjoy, appreciate, and find renewal in the natural world.

Little Erick was hungry and scared. There was more snow in Owl Creek Valley than ever before. Even his mighty father, Elijah, with his strong, sharp hooves, couldn't dig through to the delicious grasses beneath the snow. His family of elk was getting weaker every day.

"It's not fair!" cried Erick. "The snow is so deep, I can barely walk. I'm tired, and I want to eat *NOW*!"

His father turned to him and replied, "Erick, this has been a difficult winter for all the animals around here. You are not the only one who is hungry. I must go now and try to find food for all of us."

As Erick watched Elijah move slowly down the mountain, he felt sorry about what he had said to his father. He looked forward to the day when he could go with Elijah and help search for food.

Erick curled up under a Gamble's Oak tree to rest. He began to wonder what the other animals who lived around him were eating during this long and snowy winter. Suddenly, a Steller's Jay soared down from the clear, blue sky and landed on a branch above Erick.

"Hello, down there," squawked Jay. "I don't mean to frighten you, little guy, but I'm looking for my dinner, and you might be lying on it."

"How could I be lying on your dinner? Besides, I'm Erick, not little guy," snapped Erick, as he jumped to his feet.

"Well, you see, Erick, the warmth of your body on the snow melts tiny openings just big enough for my beak to reach in and pull out some nuts or berries," answered Jay. "Usually I can spot my dinner from these tree branches but not THIS snowy winter."

Erick moved aside, exposing a melted spot just like Jay had described!

"Thanks for helping me out," called Jay as he swooped down to the ground. He snatched up some dried berries in his beak and then flew off to the next grove of trees in search of more food.

Erick wondered if he could find food there also. He dug down under the snow with his little hooves, but all he felt was more cold, wet snow. Oh, how he wished his father would come back soon!

Just then he thought he saw a round bush slowly moving past him. He was so curious to find out just what it was, that he touched it with his hoof. Suddenly, Erick jumped back. He felt several, sharp needle-like pricks on his leg.

"Yikes, that hurt! You're not a bush! You're some kind of roly-poly creature!" exclaimed Erick.

"I beg your pardon, but I'm Pokey," said the large, slow-moving porcupine. "I'm on my way to eat some pine bark in that big tree over there. Sorry about my quills in your leg, but that's the only way I can protect myself."

"Well, I guess I know why you're called Pokey," muttered Erick as he tried to pull out the sharp quills with his teeth.

"The ranch dog, Tucker, has run home with a face full of my quills more than once," Pokey chuckled to himself as he waddled slowly toward his dinner.

Erick was still looking for his food when he came upon little Delbert Deer eating with his mother, Dottie.

"Excuse me," called Erick, "but what's that you're eating?"

"Why, this is a serviceberry bush," replied Dottie, as she continued chewing on the tender branches.

"Let me try that," said Erick as he bit into the small, round, frozen buds on the branch.

"*YUK!* It tastes awful! I couldn't eat that if my life depended on it." Erick cringed while spitting out a mouthful of the bitter-tasting branch.

"Well, Erick," Dottie replied, "our lives do depend on eating it, and any other shrub or small tree around here this winter. We much prefer the delicate flowers in Rancher Tom's garden in the summer, but now we have to eat what's above the snow. You'd better get used to eating things that might not be to your liking, Erick. Your life could depend on it also."

"I just passed by a group of small aspen trees just Delbert's size over by the ranch house. Maybe you'd like to feed on them," suggested Erick.

"Why, thank you, Erick. Let's go Delbert. Dinner is waiting," called Dottie.

Suddenly, Elijah appeared from over the high snowy ridge. He walked very slowly up the steep hill to where his family waited. The hard work of hunting for food had made him extremely tired. Erick watched as Elijah stopped walking. Slowly he tilted his head way back. With his mouth wide open, and using all his strength, he made a loud bugling, bellowing sound that said, *"I have found food!"*

"Yea!" squealed Erick. "My tummy was really starting to growl!"

"Sh-h-h," whispered his mother, Ellen. "It's important to listen carefully to your father."

"Follow me in a single line down to the horse pasture," Elijah instructed his family. "Rancher Tom has just put out hay for the horses. I could even smell the sweet scent of the dried alfalfa that we love to feed on in the summer. I will wait by the pasture fence until you have all safely jumped it." He then began to lead his weak and hungry family down the snow-packed trail.

As Erick was waiting for his turn at the back of the line, he was startled by a loud, plopping sound not far from him in the snow.

"Mother, who is that, and what is she doing?" inquired Erick.

"That's Feebie Fox. She jumps up like that when she is hunting and about to catch something," said Ellen.

"Hey, be quiet!" scolded Feebie. "You scared away my dinner. I was just about to catch a vole."

"What's a vole?" asked Erick.

"A vole is a delicious little mouse-like animal that lives under the blanket of soft snow. Voles are very fast, so I have to be quiet to outsmart them. The deep snow has made hunting very difficult for me. Look, Erick, I'd like to visit, but my family is waiting for dinner back in our den, and I have work to do," said Feebie as she jumped again at the sound of a vole.

"Well, we are just passing by on our way to dinner in the horse pasture. Go back to your hunting and we won't bother you," Erick replied as he and his mother kept walking.

"Who-o-o, who-o-o," came a mysterious sound above Erick.

"Who? Well, I'm Erick. Who are you?" Erick stopped and looked up at the large yellow-eyed bird.

"No, silly, I didn't ask who you are," answered Ollie, the Great Horned Owl, as he fluttered down on an old fence post. "I was calling to my mate to tell her I just caught a snowshoe hare for dinner."

"Wow, Ollie, you're so big, but I didn't even hear you coming," sighed Erick.

"That's because I have feathers with fringed edges that allow air to pass through silently. I can swoop down to the ground and quietly catch just about anything without being heard," Ollie proudly replied.

Erick wanted to ask Ollie more questions, but heard his mother call, "Erick, let's go. You will be the last one to go over the fence. Your father and I will stand there to help you if you need it."

When the elk were a short distance from the ranch road and it looked safe from all sides, they started running with enough speed to jump the fence. Inside the pasture, the horses were enjoying their dinner and didn't pay any attention to the elk.

Finally it was Erick's turn.

"I can make it," whispered Erick to himself. "I have to make it." He wanted so badly to do what his big brothers and sisters had already done.

Ellen called encouragingly, "Run, Erick! You can do it!"

"Jump!" Elijah shouted at the same time.

Erick looked straight ahead and concentrated very hard. He knew he had to clear the top of the tall fence. After taking a deep breath, he ran as fast as his little legs could go and jumped.

Suddenly he was in the horse pasture! Erick felt very proud of himself.

There was not a lot of extra food for the elk, but it was more than they had eaten in a long time.

Erick noticed two horses who were eating together.

"Hello, my name is Erick. May I eat some of your hay? I'm very hungry," he whispered softly.

"I'm Dudley," replied the black horse. "And this is my girlfriend, Murdock." His head motioned toward the plump brown horse who was eating beside him. "Please help yourself, Erick. We are very fortunate as Rancher Tom feeds us hay twice a day."

"Oh, thank you," said Erick, as he began to eat the sweet hay. He thought how lucky the horses were to have Rancher Tom.

Erick ate until his little tummy was full, and then he lay down under the silvery moon and slept with the friendly horses and his family.

In the morning, just as the sun was coming up, the elk jumped back over the fence and headed up into the woods. Erick scampered past his brothers and sisters in search of his father.

"Father," gasped Erick. "I have something important to tell you."

Erick reported to Elijah about all he had learned from his new friends and how he had even been able to help some of them find food. Elijah was very pleased.

That evening as the elk herd came back to the ranch, again looking for food, Erick walked alongside his father. As Erick and Elijah looked across the ranch road into the pasture, they saw not only hay for the horses but several extra bales spread out on the glistening moonlit snow. Erick realized at that moment that Rancher Tom was helping his family also. This time it was Erick's little head that tilted back and with all his might he gave out a squeaky, bellowing sound that said, *"We have found food!"*

Elijah looked down with great pride at little Erick and invited him to help lead their family down the snowy path to dinner.

| | | | | | | |
|---|---|---|---|---|---|---|
| **Elk** | **Snowshoe Hare** | **Chipmunk** | **Vole** | **Steller's Jay** | **Black Bear** | **Great Horned Owl** |

| | |
|---|---|
| **Elk** | travel from high mountains to low valleys and gather in large herds before winter arrives. The males are called bulls and the females are called cows. The males grow new antlers (hard bony growths on their heads) every year which fall off in early spring. New and larger antlers then begin to grow. Elk once lived in every state, but because they were hunted so widely, they are now found only in and west of the Rocky Mountains. The bugle sound they make is a bark-like warning with a strange, high-pitched squeal. Elk have a dark brown coat of hair in the summer. In autumn, they molt (shed) their hair and grow a thick grayish-brown coat for the winter. |
| **Snowshoe Hares** | are brown in the summer, but they turn white in the winter. This change of color for protection is called camouflage. When they are white, they are difficult to see in the snow, but they leave a trail of footprints. |
| **Chipmunks** | hibernate (sleep deeply in the winter) for short periods of time. They wake up only to eat some food they have stored in their dugout homes under the snow, then they go back to sleep until spring arrives. |
| **Voles** | are very much like mice, except they have shorter noses and tails. They eat grass, seeds, roots and twig bark. |
| **Steller's Jays** | live in the mountains, mostly in the forests. They are not afraid of people. If you are having a picnic in the mountains, they may try to steal your food. |
| **Black Bears** | also hibernate after eating great quantities of food in the fall. A thick layer of fat forms under their hides to keep them warm all winter. They sleep from three to five months, but awaken easily in warm weather and may even leave their dens for brief periods of time. |
| **Great Horned Owls** | sleep all day and hunt by night. The pointed feathers on their heads look like ears or horns. Owls can swivel their heads around to look behind them. They blend in with the color of tree bark. Owls have very keen eyesight. They eat small animals and birds. |

# OWL CREEK VALLEY

**Deer**     **Porcupine**     **Ermine**     **Beaver**     **Red Fox**     **Ptarmigan**     **Mountain Lion**

| | |
|---|---|
| **Deer** | are the most common wild animals in America today. Baby deer are called fawns. Deer are related to elk, moose and caribou. |
| **Porcupines** | are nocturnal (they come out at night) and spend the day in a hollowed-out tree or rocky den. Their favorite food is the bark of trees. When they eat the bark all around the tree, the tree is destroyed. Their bodies are covered with long, very sharp quills which protect them from other animals. |
| **Ermine** | are members of the weasel family. Their coats are white in the winter and brown in the summer. They eat small rodents and cottontail rabbits. Sometimes they feed on the antlers that fall off deer and elk. |
| **Beavers** | are great builders. Their homes are called lodges. They are made of sticks and mud and are found in or near water. Beavers live inside their lodges throughout the winter. They also build dams (barriers made up of limbs and logs). |
| **Red Foxes** | are members of the canine family, which includes wolves, coyotes, jackals, and dogs. They have large bushy tails with white tips, and black ears and feet. The females look after their pups (babies) until they are old enough to hunt and survive alone. |
| **Ptarmigan** | are birds that have a covering of feathers on their feet to help them travel across the deep snow. Like the ermine and snowshoe hare they also change their color to white in the winter for protection. |
| **Mountain Lions** | (or pumas) are large members of the cat family. They can weigh up to 200 pounds. They have very strong paws and they walk on their toes with the back part of their feet raised. Mountain lion's diets include mostly deer, rabbits and birds and occasionally weak, old elk. |

*All these animals share a habitat of great natural beauty. People like to live in the same beautiful areas as the animals in this story do. When the land becomes too crowded, animals are forced to move to other places where there might not be enough food for them. It is important to preserve wildlife habitat by keeping open natural spaces so that future generations can enjoy this beautiful environment also.*

If you would like to learn more about our animal neighbors and what you can do to help them, here are some suggestions:

❖ Visit your local nature center to learn more about the animals where you live.

❖ Put out a bird feeder and keep it filled all winter long.

❖ Join organizations that protect wildlife and participate in their programs.

❖ Read nature books and magazines that include stories about animals.

❖ Help protect wildlife and natural habitats where you live.

❖ Watch nature programs on television.

❖ Visit natural history museums.